THE WIZARD OF OP
by ed emberley

LITTLE, BROWN & CO.   BOSTON · TORONTO

P

LIBRARY OF CONGRESS CATALOGING IN PUBLICATION DATA

EMBERLEY, ED.
"THE WIZARD OF OP."

SUMMARY: A SLIGHTLY INEPT WIZARD CASTS HIS SPELLS
WHICH ARE DEMONSTRATED TO US THROUGH THE TECHNIQUES
OF OPTICAL ART.
[1.MAGICIANS-- FICTION] I.TITLE
PZ7.E565WI [E]   75-20345
ISBN 0-316-23610-1

FIRST EDITION
T 10/75

PUBLISHED SIMULTANEOUSLY
IN CANADA BY
LITTLE, BROWN AND COMPANY
(CANADA) LIMITED—

PRINTED IN THE UNITED STATES OF AMERICA

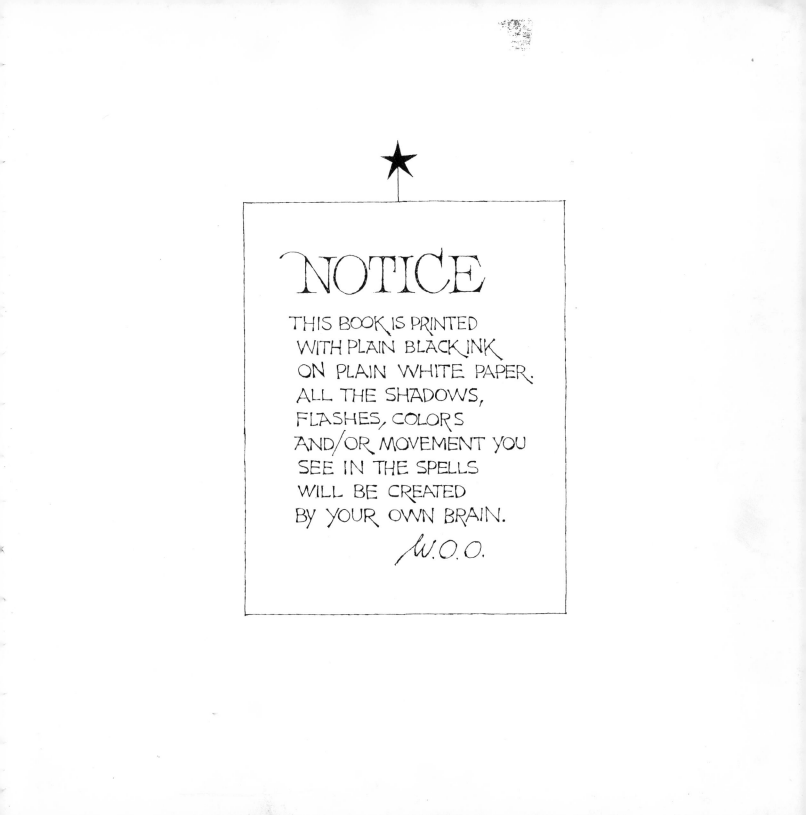

NOTICE

THIS BOOK IS PRINTED
WITH PLAIN BLACK INK
ON PLAIN WHITE PAPER.
ALL THE SHADOWS,
FLASHES, COLORS
AND/OR MOVEMENT YOU
SEE IN THE SPELLS
WILL BE CREATED
BY YOUR OWN BRAIN.

W.O.O.

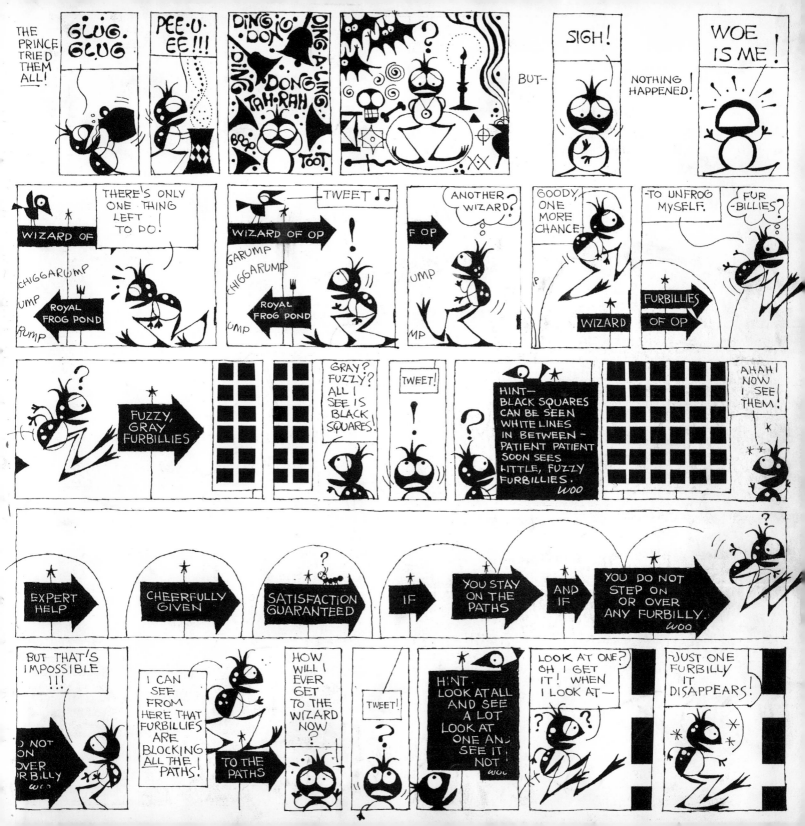

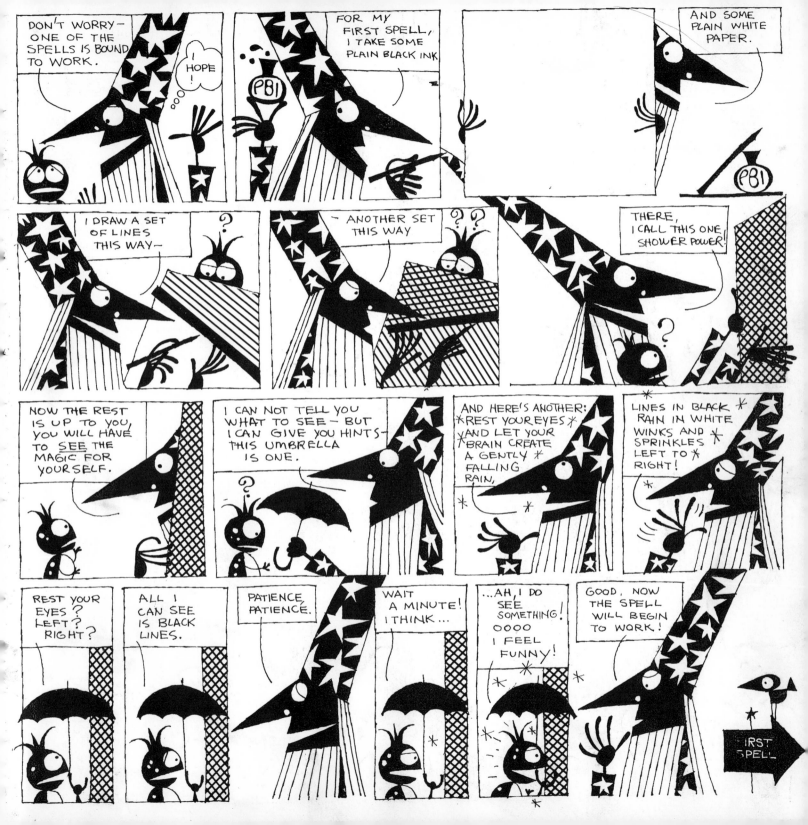

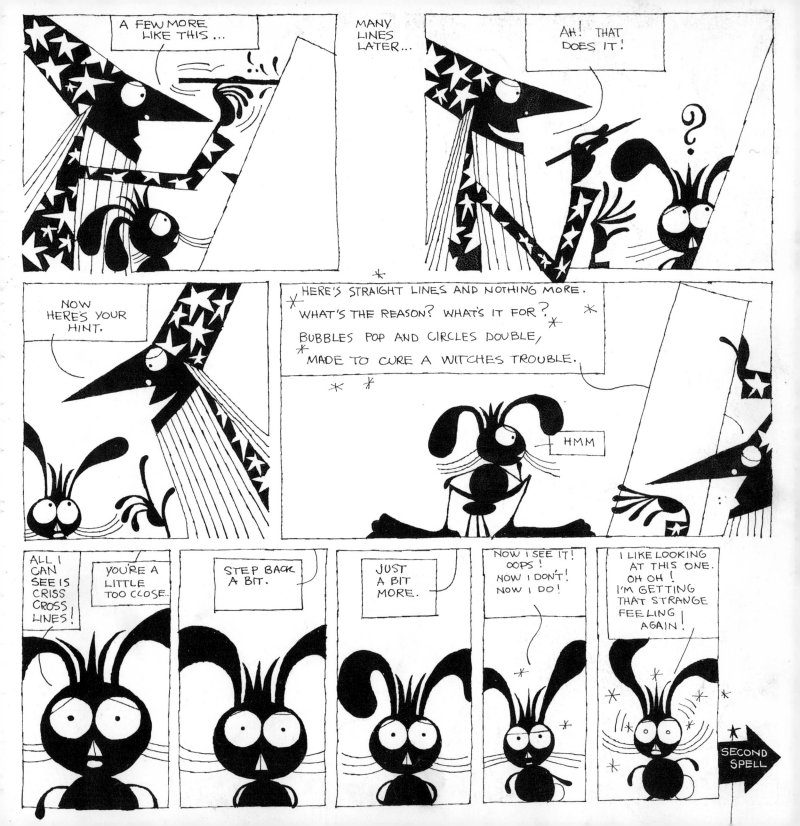

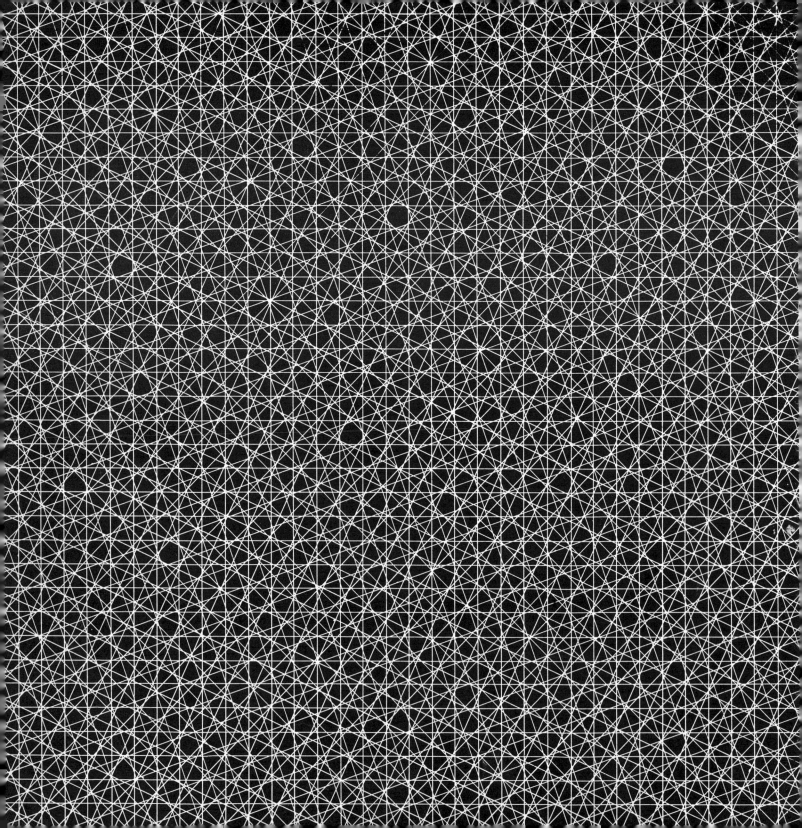

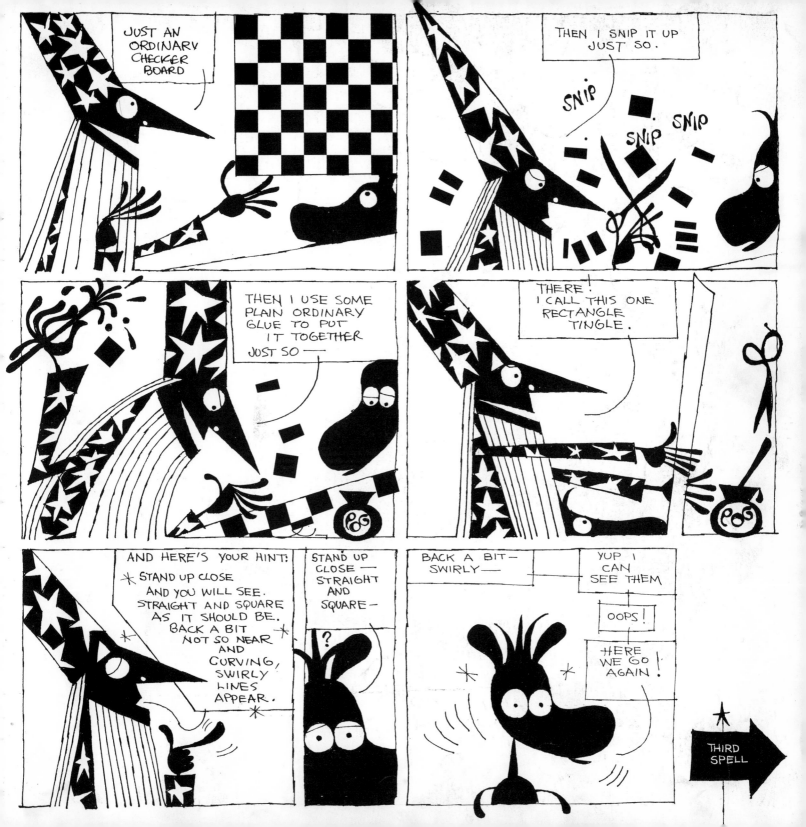

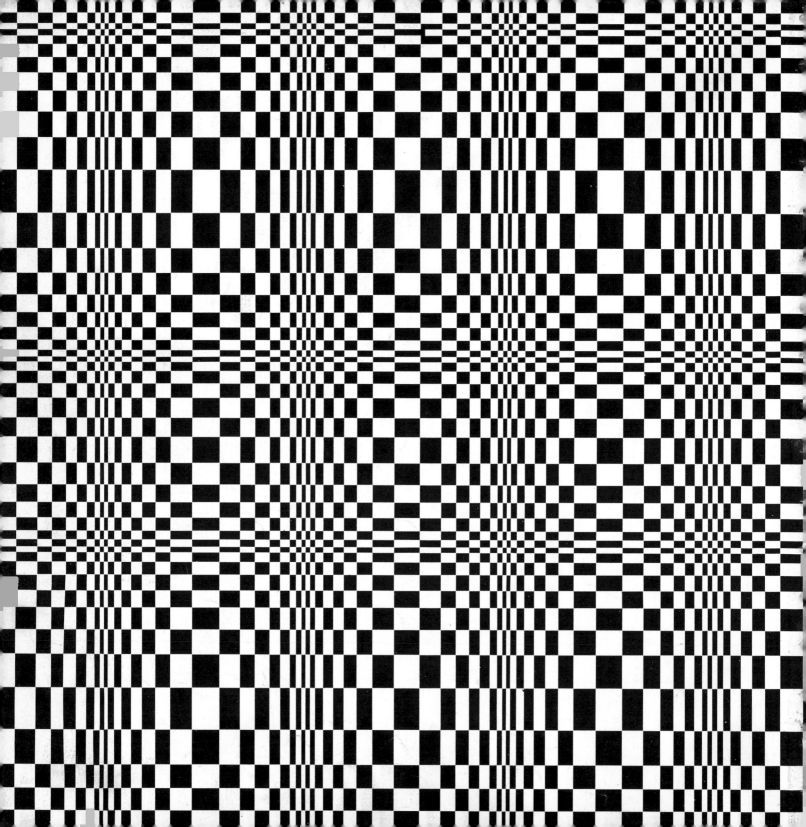

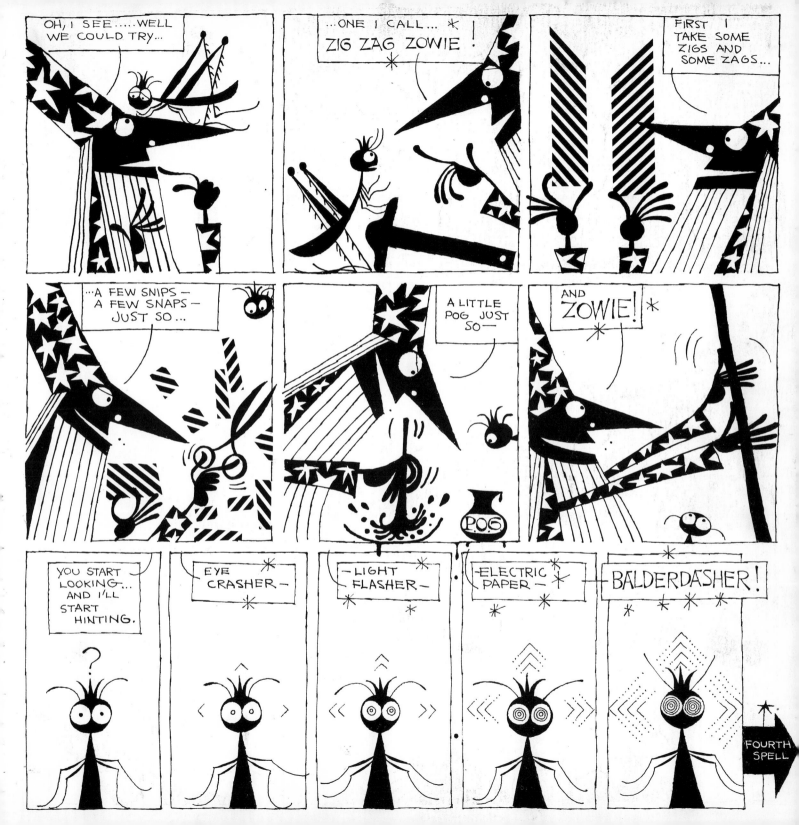

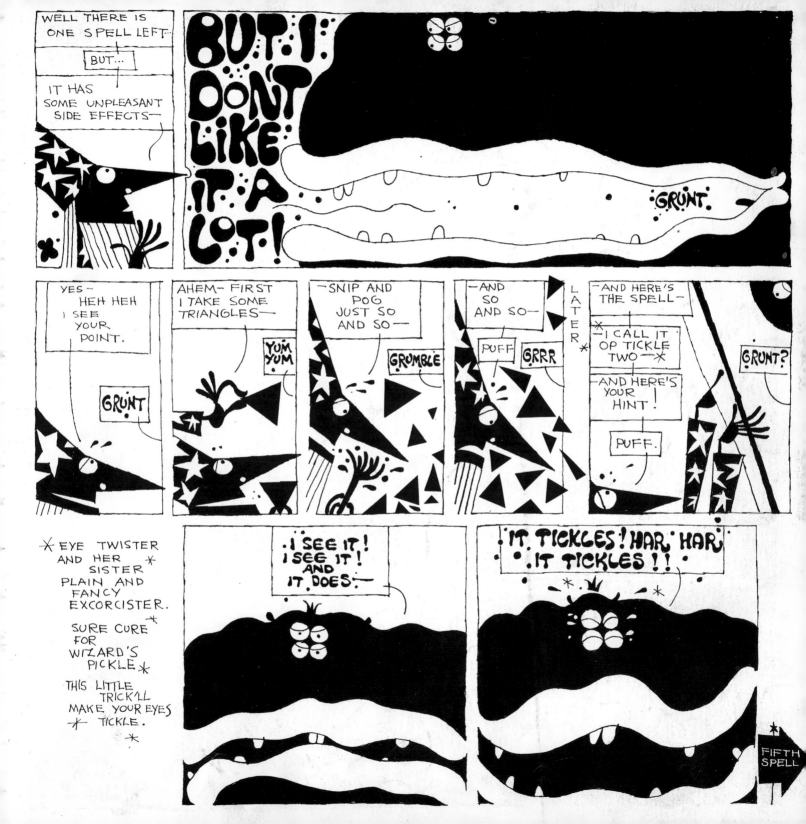

YOU WILL SEE SOME MAGIC THERE. — WOO

*✲ TO SEE THE MAGIC — COME CLOSE — LOOK INTO MY EYES — TAKE THE BOOK AND MOVE IT AROUND IN SMALL CIRCLES.